Discovering
SHARLIE

Discovering
SHARLIE

Case of the Missing Sea Serpent

Craig Vroom

illustrated by Linn Trochim

Tru Publishing
2939 S Mayflower Way
Boise, ID 83709

Published by Tru Publishing. No part of this book may be reproduced or transmitted in any form or by any means, electronic or mechanical, including photocopying, recording, or by any information storage and retrieval system, without written permission from the publisher. For more information, address Tru Publishing, 2939 S Mayflower Way, Boise ID 83709. Visit the Tru Publishing website at www.TruPublishing.com

Library of Congress Control Number: 2015952205
ISBN (paperback): 978-1-941420-11-9
ISBN (hardcover): 978-1-941420-12-6

1 2 3 4 5 6 19 18 17 16 15
1st edition, September 2015

Printed in the United States of America

Cover and Interior Design — Tru Publishing
www.trupublishing.com

Editing — Robin Bethel
www.prosestudio.com

For Evan Andrew Hall,
and to his spirit of adventure.

Olivia, the girl, most knowing and wise,
Squinted and rubbed her bluish-green eyes.
Through the mist of the lake she could barely make out
What looked like a colorful sea serpent's snout.

Could this be so? Could this be true?
Could a sea serpent live beside me, beside you?

But before this great sighting, let's go back in time.
Back to a place: to the scene of the crime.

"Olivia! Scotland Yard's on the phone!
A guy named Inspector Angus MacClone."

MacClone, the detective, worked for queens and for kings.
A Scot who could solve most mysterious things.
But this case was full of questions and doubt.
So he called for assistance — to figure it out.

"Olivia, me lass, we need you up here!
We haven't seen Nessie for many a year.
Our Loch Ness Monster disappeared in bad weather.
And, since then, we've searched all the lakes and through heather."

When Olivia hung up, she turned to her mate
Her friend who she sometimes called "Jenny, the Great."
"They've lost their dear Nessie — in the fog and the mist.
It sounds like he really could use an assist."

Jenny and "Liv" were the best of detectives
Their clients had rated them "Highly Effective!"
They could size something up with the smartest of smarts
And know the direction, deep down in their hearts,
That they needed to go — to find a solution
And bring a tough case to a final conclusion.

Then Olivia cried out: "Our Dolphin MacBlast!
It can zig to the future! It can zag to the past!
This super, transducer, transforming contraption
Can take us to places with all of the action!

We can swim like a fish or fly like a rocket.
And my brown Lucky Penny that I'll put in my pocket,
Will keep us from harm, through time and through trouble,
And will get us to Scotland and back on the double."

So the Blaster figured the time and the place
And it zoomed them right off without leaving a trace.
Without too much trouble. Without too much fuss.
Right into a sleek, double-decker red bus!

London was rockin' — with a Twist and a Shout.
Bobbies with nightsticks were strutting about.
Big Ben was timing Beefeaters that guard.
Then, standing before them. There it was:

Scotland Yard!

"A pleasure to meet you!" said Angus MacClone.
"Much better in person than over the phone!"
He showed them a picture.   She was longish and green.
"And this is the very last place she was seen!"

"The lake is real deep and it's easy to hide.
That's why Nessie…" MacClone got real quiet and sighed.
"You've just got to find her!" he said through his tears.
"She hasn't been spotted in three or four years."

Yes, this would be a most difficult case.
So they took off for Loch Ness. Off to the place
Where Nessie had lived. Where her sightings were news.
And set about searching for leads and for clues.

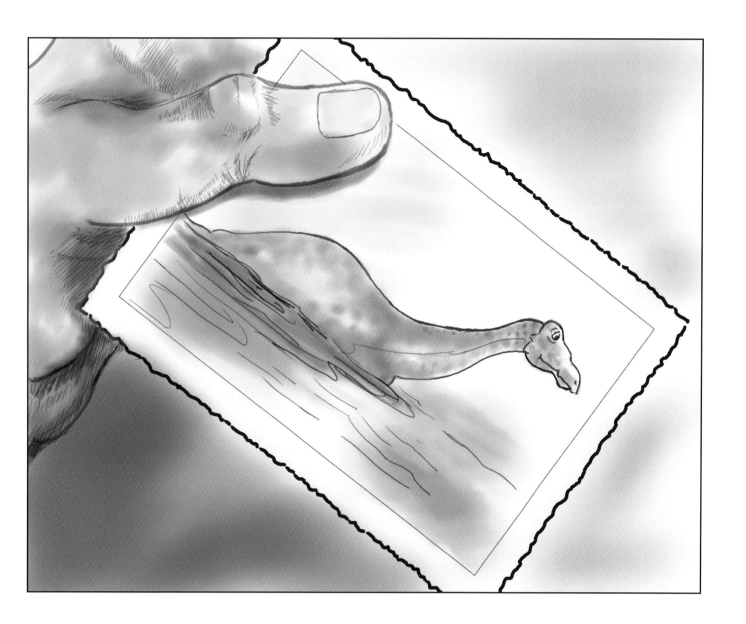

"The Blaster can find her!" Liv said with a smile.
"We'll search high and low, every inch, every mile!
Let me just enter the undersea code,
Changing the Blaster to Submarine mode."

Gluggity-glug. The girls started diving.
Jenny was searching. Olivia driving.
They searched for five hours. At fast and slow speeds.
But no sign of Nessie, just catfish and reeds.

Where did she go, without leaving a trace?
They surfaced the Blaster to return to their base.
"Hey Olivia!" yelled Jenny, her voice full of hope.
"Here's something to see on the Search-a-ma-scope.

Look at that sign! By the mouth of that river.
It says: SEA CREATURES ZOO
Owner: Dougal MacLiver."
"Hmmmm," said Olivia. "Let's pull up to his dock!
We'll see if MacLiver is willing to talk."

13

MacLiver looked dirty and shifty and mean.
He had a thin mustache, all mildewed and green.
His head kind of bobbled from the east to the south.
And spittle came out from the side of his mouth.

"I've got big bluish whales. Fast, flying fish.
Aberdeen Albacore who eat from a dish.
Highlander Herrings, that really get messy.
But I've never, not ever, had a creature named Nessie."

MacLiver must have thought they were dumber than fools.
It was time to investigate his cages and pools.
"Thanks, Dougal," said Olivia. "We'll be on our way.
You and your creatures have a wonderful day!"

"That low-life was lying," Jenny said in a rage.
"I'll bet he's got Nessie locked up in a cage!"
So the Blaster was set to go down real steep.
To find "little" Nessie they would have to go deep.

The Blaster was quiet — all you heard was a "swish."
Searching for places that might have big fish.

Creepity creep.
Deepity deep.

Soon they saw cages, and just up ahead
Was an Outlander Orca with kelp for a bed.
"We're looking for Nessie! Is she down in this jail?"
Sheila, the Orca, began telling her tale.

"Nessie was kidnapped by Dougal MacLiver!
He's a really bad man!" she said, with a shiver.
"He kept her locked up — kept her quiet and hid her.
Was selling her off to the most-highest bidder.

So she cut through her cage with her teeth. She was brave!
And disappeared into that brownish-green cave!"

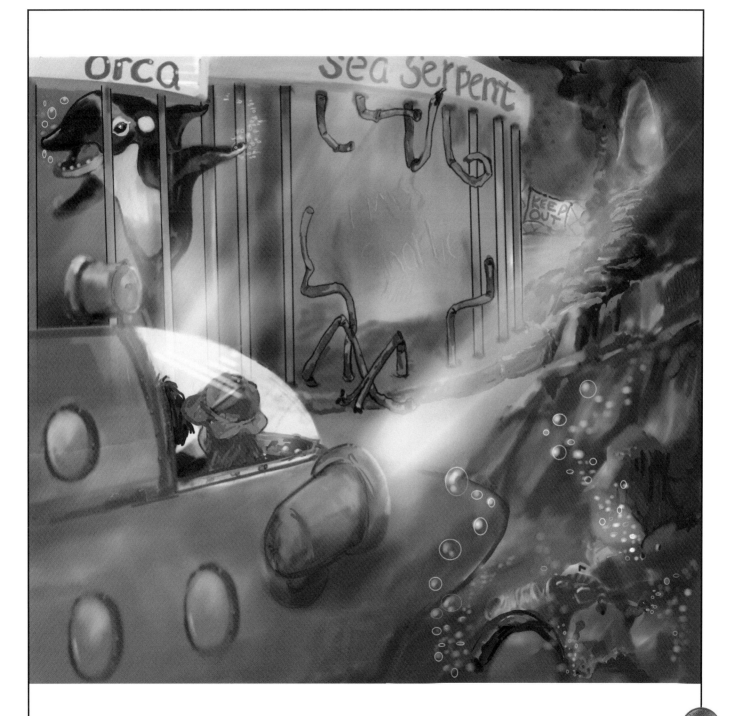

19

Into the brownish-green cave went the Blaster.
Sucked into a swirl going faster and faster.
Swirling and swirling, round and around.

Tumbling,

tumbling,

tumbling down.

Caught up in a vortex. From the east to the west.
The Blaster's machinery put to the test.
Their compass and gauges were spinning about.
Outside looked in! Inside looked out!

Faster they sped along old lava caves.
Pushed through great caverns by gigantic waves.

"It's hard to believe!" Jenny turned in her chair.
"The Little Lost River is just over there!
And now we are passing — we'll get there real soon —
Some black, crusty craters ... just like the Moon!"

"The needle is moving back and then forth.
It reads, 113 West and 44 North!"

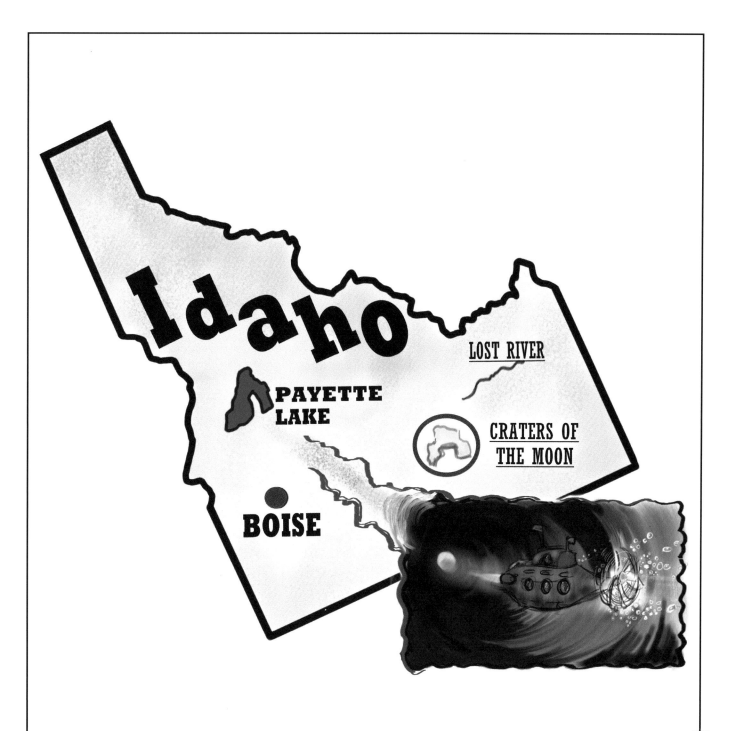

Idaho

PAYETTE
LAKE

LOST RIVER

CRATERS OF
THE MOON

BOISE

The Blaster was slowing, down to a crawl.
"We've landed in Idaho! A place named McCall!"
Then up, they went up. Liv took off the brake.
And they shot to the top of a beautiful lake.

Their scope kind of sputtered — and then came back on.
Pinks and light blues were breaking at dawn.

Reflected in water that looked calm as glass
Were Tamarack Trout and Bitterroot Bass.

A Payette-Lake osprey swooping up toward its nest.
Idaho scenery at its beautiful best.

Then Olivia, the girl, all knowing and wise,
Squinted and rubbed her bluish-green eyes.
Through the mist of the lake she could barely make out
What looked like a colorful, sea serpent's snout.

Or could it have been a gigantic snake?
Or a rather large sturgeon on top of the lake?

The creature inched closer. Moving out from the shade.
It started to swim toward the girls, unafraid.
Its head had some yellow, some pink, and some green.
Its front teeth were silver. Its tail long and lean.

It wiggled and squiggled and giggled along.
And it sounded as if it was humming a song.
"Hmmm Ackle!" — now like a cackling hen.
"Hmmm Ackle!" it cackled — the noise once again.

The girls set the Blaster for their current location.
And the Idaho EarTube for "Serpent Translation."

"I'm Sharlie!" it gurgled. "I live in McCall.
My mother's the most famous serpent of all.
We once lived in Scotland — a place called Loch Ness
Back in an era — a time, more or less —
When we serpents were plentiful, roaming the seas,
And just having fun in the sun, if you please.

But then came the ice age, wiping most of us out.
The few of us left were just drifting about
'Til the underground rivers and their vortex and wake
Brought us right here — to this luminous lake.

We love it right here, my mother and I,
Frolicking under the Idaho sky.

But Mom would get lonesome for her Auntie MacFlow
So she'd swim back to Scotland, every ten years or so,
'Til that scoundrel, MacLiver, and his nasty old crew,
Trapped her and caged her in that horrible zoo."

"You know the rest, she escaped back to stay.
Here's where we'll live. And here's where we'll play.
Some children will see us. We'll sometimes appear.
Especially if they believe that we're here.

As for MacClone, don't tell him you know.
And Nessie and I will stay safe down below."

"Don't worry," said Olivia. "Your wish will come true.
You serpents will never be caged in a zoo!
It's our little secret, for Jenny and me.
Keeping you safe for all children to see."

So the next time you go to the lake clear and blue,
Keep your eye out for Sharlie.

She's got her eye out for you.

About the Author
Craig Vroom

Author Craig Vroom writes adventure stories for children. He enjoys visiting classrooms at all grade levels, showing students how reading and writing poetry can be a fun and enriching experience. He has been invited to present and sign his books at many venues, including the AuthorFest of the Rockies and The Baseball Hall of Fame in Cooperstown, NY.

"I love the Idaho outdoor experience: the mountains, the wildlife, and the beautiful lakes. I thought that with *Discovering Sharlie: Case of the Missing Sea Serpent*, we could combine a spirit of mystique and adventure with some of those wonderful Idaho experiences." Vroom lives in the west-central mountains of Idaho.

About the Illustrator
Linn Trochim

Linn started her career in the film animation industry in Hollywood, drawing famous characters for Hanna-Barbera Studios. She has illustrated many forms of media, but her true love is illustrating for children. Linn collaborated with Mr. Vroom on three other children's adventure books, including:

The Secretous Sign,

The Riddle of Shipwreck Sound, and

The Tall Trees.

CPSIA information can be obtained at www.ICGtesting.com
Printed in the USA
LVIW01n1215161115
462224LV00001B/2